MAX EXPLAINS EVERYTHING

GROCERY STORE EXPERT

STACY McANULTY

ILLUSTRATED BY
DEBORAH HOCKING

G. P. PUTNAM'S SONS

For my aunts, all of them: Eva, Betty Ann, Ruby, Bonnie & Carol.—S.McA.

For Jay, who is, quite simply, the best.—D.H.

G. P. PUTNAM'S SONS
an imprint of Penguin Random House LLC
375 Hudson Street
New York, NY 10014

G. P. Putnam's Sons is a registered trademark of Penguin Random House LLC.

Library of Congress Cataloging-in-Publication Data is available upon request.

Manufactured in China by RR Donnelley Asia Printing Solutions Ltd.
ISBN 9781101996447
10 9 8 7 6 5 4 3 2 1

Design by Marikka Tamura.
Text set in Gotham Medium.
The illustrations were created with gouache and colored pencil
on Arches watercolor paper, then digitally manipulated.

I know a lot about the grocery store.
Mom makes me go All!
The!
Time!

Like when we
run out of stuff.

Mom, we're
out of milk.
But that's okay,
I'll drink water.

Mom, we're
out of bread.
But that's okay, I'll
eat crackers.

If you don't want to go, try this.

Hide.

Fake an injury.

Ow, my pinkie toe hurts.

Hide again.

Fake a bigger injury.

Ow, my big toe hurts.

If Mom snaps her fingers and points, that means it's *really* time to go.

You're in charge of finding the perfect cart.

But your mom's in charge of picking the route.

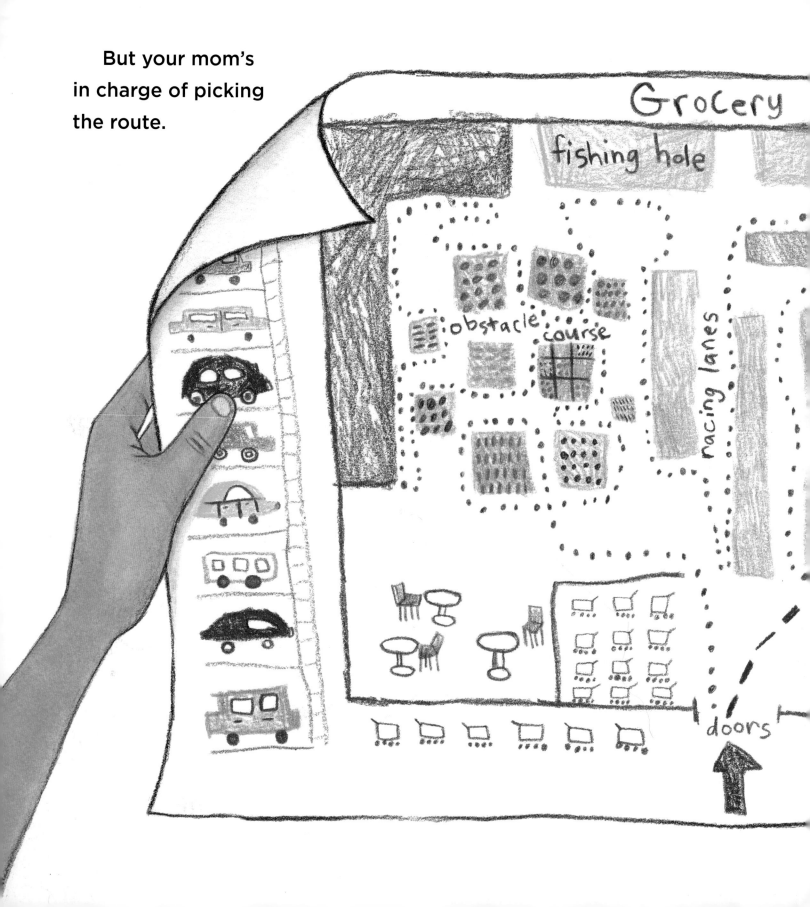

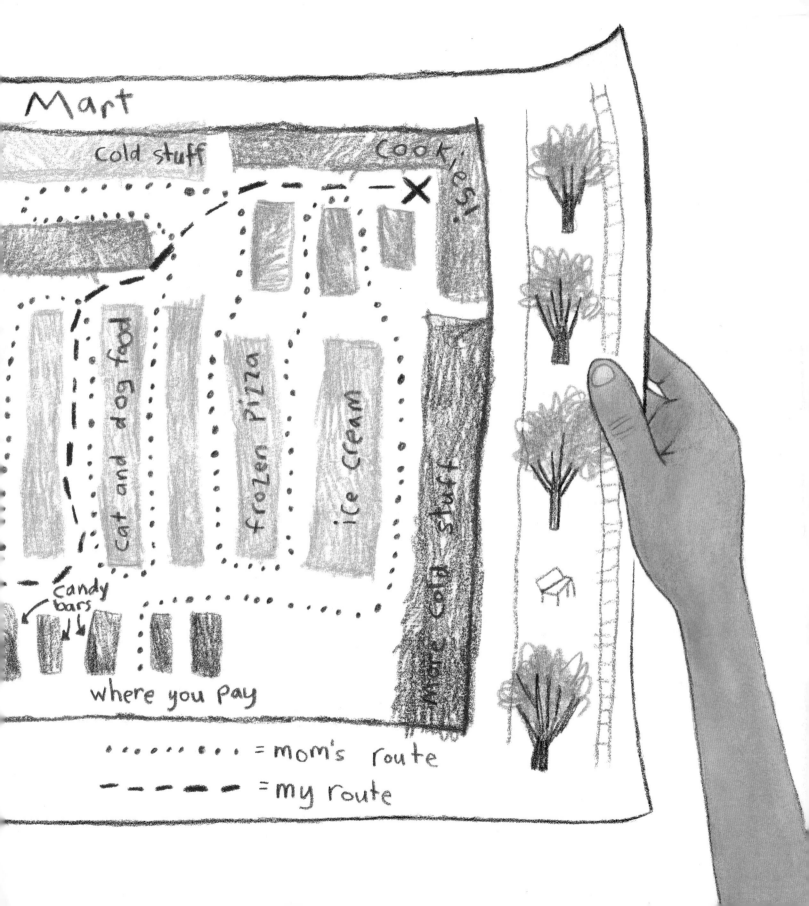

You'll probably start in the produce section, which is a good place to learn to juggle.

Just avoid an apple-lanche.

Next, you'll go fishing and you won't even need a pole.

Keep a lookout for
free samples. Everything
tastes better when served
on a toothpick.

Today's
Sample
Tofu-Seaweed
Calamari
Wraps

The store has about 8,000 aisles! If you get tired, hitch a ride.

This will speed things up!

Bye-bye, beans!

Adios, applesauce!

Catch ya later, ketchup!

Pardon me, pickles!

So long, spaghetti sauce!

But don't get too comfortable.
You need to be ready for . . .

Cereal! The fate of breakfast is in your hands.

Just hurry and choose before your mom does or else—

Maybe you didn't get the cereal you wanted,
but you can make up for it. Because next is . . .

COOKIES! Grab *all* your
favorites and then give your mom
your saddest puppy-dog eyes.

If that doesn't work,
promise to eat all your dinner,
including the green stuff.

And if that doesn't work,
promise to be the best kid ever.

And if *that* doesn't work,
promise to never, ever ask
for anything again.

Sorry,
not today.

When you get to the pet food aisle,
always grab a bag of dog food. Even if
you don't have a dog. I figure it's just
one step closer to getting one.

In the bakery, get something with frosting. Just tell your mom it's a holiday and then make one up.

It's Llama Appreciation Day. We need a cake.

I don't think so.

It's Boys Named Max Day. We need doughnuts.

Sorry, not today.

It's Opposite Day. We need cupcakes.

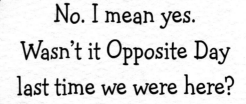

No. I mean yes. Wasn't it Opposite Day last time we were here?

At checkout, don't forget to grab some candy. (Like you need to be reminded.)

Just sneak it between the BUTTER and the BREAD. Or the CHEESE and the CHERRIES.

Or the RICE and *Ravioli.* Or the PASTA and Peas. Or the CAT FOOD and the CARROTS.

Max, we're not getting a kitten.

But I am getting a candy bar!

This is my favorite part.

And don't worry if you didn't do it all right.
You will probably have to do it again next week.
Or sooner if you forgot something.